P9-BIW-888

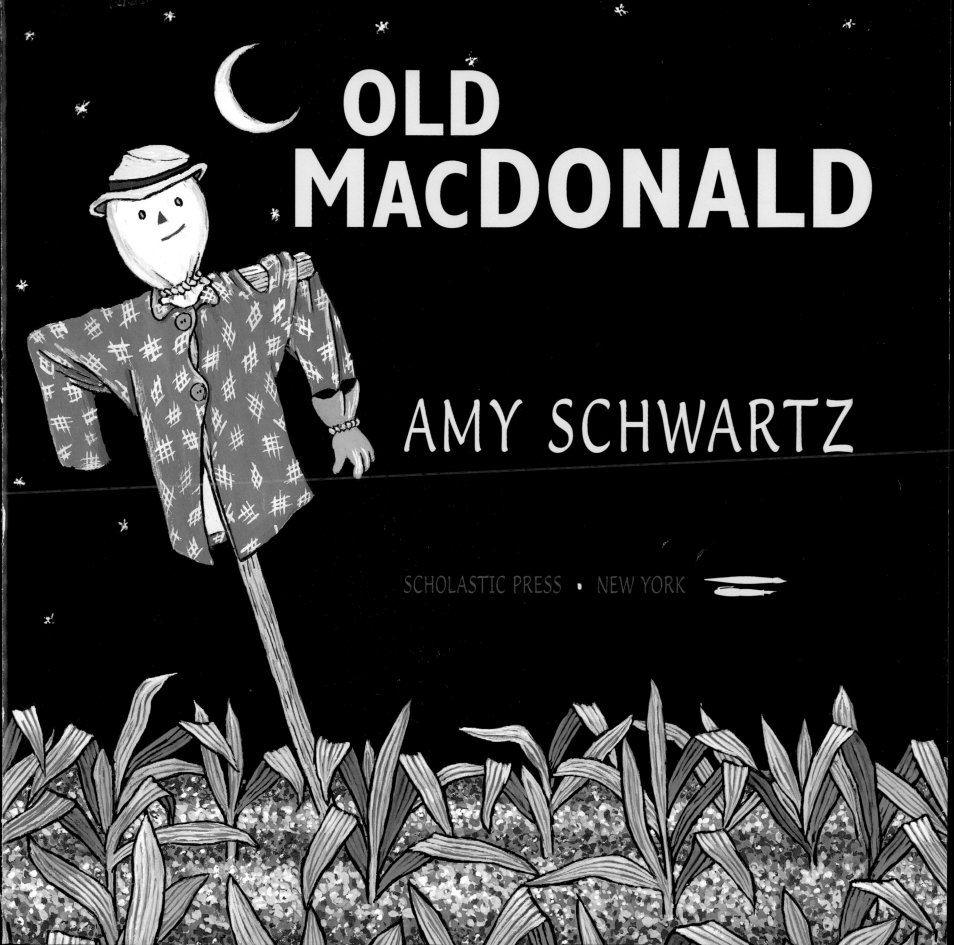

OLD MacDONALD

AMY SCHWARTZ

SCHOLASTIC PRESS · NEW YORK

LIBRARY OF CONGRESS CATALOGING-IN-PUBLICATION DATA

Schwartz, Amy
Old MacDonald / by Amy Schwartz.   p.   cm.
Summary: The inhabitants of Old MacDonald's farm are
described, verse by verse, including his tractor and his
neighbors. Music is given on the last page.
ISBN 0-590-46189-3
1. Folk songs,   English—United   States—Texas.
[1. Folk songs—United States.] 1. Title.PZ8.3.S38911501
1998 782.42162'13'0833—dc21 97-10111   CIP AC

10 9 8 7 6 5 4 3 2 1   9/9 0/0 01 02 03

Printed in Singapore 46
First edition, May 1999

The display type was set in Gill Sans Condensed Bold.
The text type was set in Lucida Casual EF,
Gill Sans Bold, and Gill Sans Condensed Bold.
Amy Schwartz's art was rendered in gouache.

for **JACOB**

Old MacDonald had a farm,
E - I - E - I - O!

And on this farm
he had a rooster,
E - I - E - I - O!
With a **cock-a-doodle** here
and a **cock-a-doodle** there.
Here a **doodle**,
there a **doodle**,
everywhere a **cock-a-doodle**.
Old MacDonald had a farm,
E - I - E - I - O!

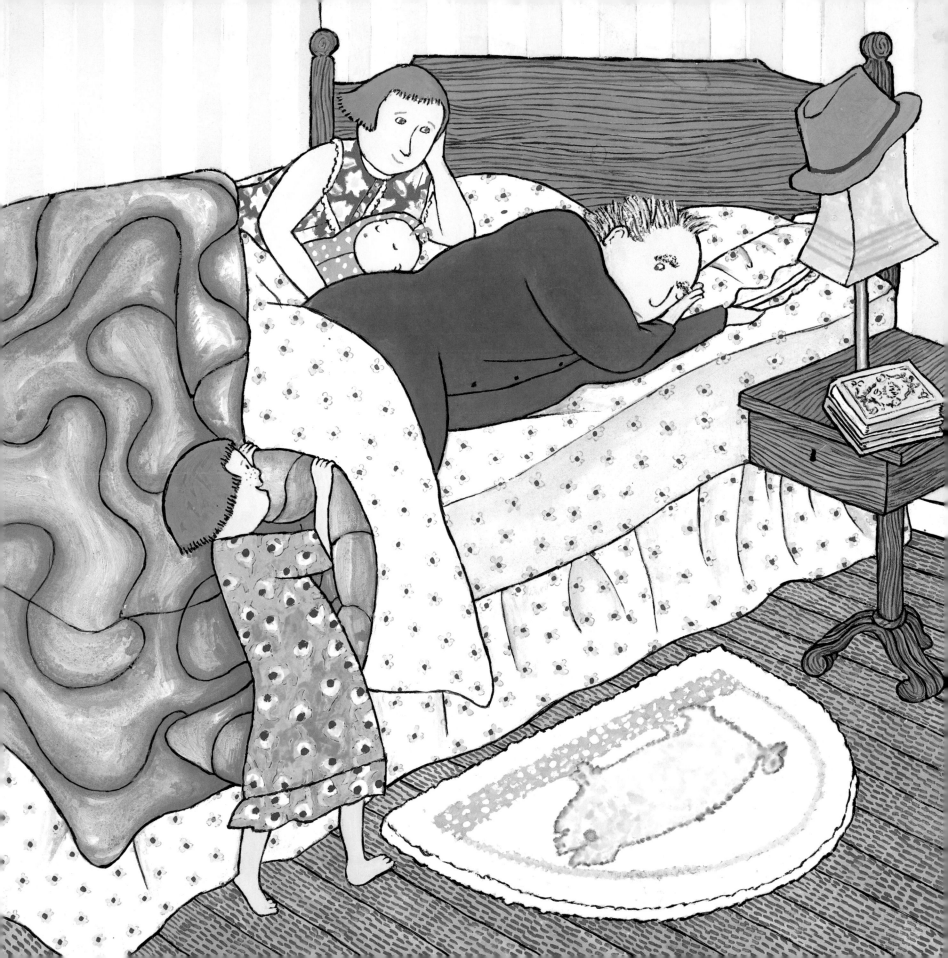

And on this farm he had some cats,

E - I - E - I - O!

With a **meow meow** here and a **meow meow** there.

Here a **meow**, there a **meow**, everywhere a **meow meow**.

Old MacDonald had a farm,

E - I - E - I - O!

And on this farm
he had some chicks,
E - I - E - I - O!
With a **cheep cheep** here
and a **cheep cheep** there.
Here a **cheep**,
there a **cheep**,
everywhere a **cheep cheep**.
Old MacDonald had a farm,
E - I - E - I - O!

And on this farm he had a cow,
E - I - E - I - O!
With a **moo moo** here
and a **moo moo** there.

Here a **moo**, there a **moo**,
everywhere a **moo moo**.
Old MacDonald had a farm,
E - I - E - I - O!

And on this farm he had a tractor,
E - I - E - I - O!
With a **putt putt** here
and a **putt putt** there.
Here a **putt**, there a **putt**,
everywhere a **putt putt**.
Old MacDonald had a farm,
E - I - E - I - O!

And on this farm
he had some sheep,
E - I - E - I - O!
With a **baa baa** here
and a **baa baa** there.
Here a **baa**,
there a **baa**,
everywhere a **baa baa**.
Old MacDonald had a farm,
E - I - E - I - O!

And on this farm he had some ducks,
E - I - E - I - O!
With a **quack quack** here
and a **quack quack** there.

Here a **quack**, there a **quack**,
everywhere a **quack quack**.
Old MacDonald had a farm,
E - I - E - I - O!

And on this farm he had a horse,
E - I - E - I - O!
With a **neigh neigh** here
and a **neigh neigh** there.
Here a **neigh**, there a **neigh**,
everywhere a **neigh neigh**.
Old MacDonald had a farm,
E - I - E - I - O!

And on this farm he had some goats,
E - I - E - I - O!
With a **maa maa** here and a **maa maa** there.
Here a **maa**, there a **maa**,
everywhere a **maa maa**.
Old MacDonald had a farm,
E - I - E - I - O!

And on this farm he had some pigs,
E - I - E - I - O!
With an **oink oink** here and an **oink oink** there.
Here an **oink**, there an **oink**,
everywhere an **oink oink**.
Old MacDonald had a farm,
E - I - E - I - O!

And on this farm he had some dogs,
E - I - E - I - O!
With a **woof woof** here and a **woof woof** there.
Here a **woof**, there a **woof**, everywhere a **woof woof**.
Old MacDonald had a farm,
E - I - E - I - O!

And on this farm he had some neighbors,
E - I - E - I - O!
With a **yakkity yak** here
and a **yakkity yak** there.
Here a **yak**, there a **yak**,
everywhere a **yakkity yak**.
Old MacDonald had a farm,
E - I - E - I - O!

And on this farm he had a song,
E - I - E - I - O!

With a **tra la la** here and a **tra la la** there.

Here a **la**, there a **la**, everywhere a **tra la la**.

Old MacDonald had a farm,
E - I - E - I - O!

Old MacDonald Had a Farm

Starting with the rooster, follow the animals clockwise to cue the next verse of the song.